"Come on, team. It's game time!" —Charlie Brown

Library of Congress Control Number 2014947580
ISBN 978-1-62157-259-6

Published in the United States by
Little Patriot Press
An imprint of Regnery Publishing
A Salem Communications Company
300 New Jersey Ave NW
Washington, DC 20001
www.RegneryKids.com
www.Peanuts.com

Manufactured in the United States of America
10 9 8 7 6 5 4 3 2 1

Books are available in quantity for promotional or premium use.
For information on discounts and terms, please visit our website: www.Regnery.com.

Distributed to the trade by
Perseus Distribution
250 West 57th Street
New York, NY 10107

Who Cares, Charlie Brown?

Peanuts created by **Charles M. Schulz**

Written by **Diane Lindsey Reeves** and **Cheryl Shaw Barnes**

Illustrated by **Tom Brannon**

Little Patriot Press

It's the biggest game of the season! Last year, Charlie Brown's team lost against Peppermint Patty's team 112 to 0.

This year things were going to be different.
They just couldn't lose by that much again.

"Come on, team," Charlie Brown said. "It's
game time!"

Charlie Brown was the team manager, and it was his job to get the field ready. "Snoopy, chalk the field!"

"Woodstock, dust the bases!"

"Sally, fill the water bucket!"

Sally picked up the BIG bucket and headed to the
water fountain WAY on the other side of the field.

"There must be a law against bossing little sisters around so much," Sally complained to Franklin.

"Who knows? Maybe there is," Franklin slurped a big drink of water. "They made a law so we could share the same water fountain."

Huh? What was Franklin talking about?

Franklin explained that things were different when his grandfather was a boy. Black people were not allowed to drink from the same water fountains as white people. They couldn't eat at the same restaurants, or even sit in the front seats of buses.

"But that's ridiculous!" Sally exclaimed. "Why should the outside matter? It's the inside that counts!"

Franklin agreed. "That's what Martin Luther King Jr. said. He dreamed of the day when his children would be judged by their character, not by the color of their skin."

"I have a dream too," Sally confided with a playful wink. "I dream that our team beats your team today!"

Sally's dream didn't exactly come true. But it wasn't the complete nightmare Charlie Brown had feared. Peppermint Patty's team was only up by 59 at the bottom of the ninth. Things were looking up.

CRACK!

Schroeder was on first base. Sally was on second. There was still one out left, and Linus was up to bat.

Linus made two strikes before—WHAM! He nearly knocked the ball out of the park.

"Run, Linus, run!" his team cheered.

Linus ran to first base.
Schroeder moved up to second.

Charlie Brown was cheering Sally on to third base
when the ball whizzed by his head.

Startled, he jumped back, got tangled in his shoelaces, and THUMP!

Sally was safe. Charlie Brown was out.

"Charlie Brown! Are you okay?" Linus put his blanket under Charlie Brown's head.

"Who do you think you are?" Lucy snapped. "Clara Barton?"

"Would that be so bad?" Linus asked his big sister. "After all, Clara Barton is famous for starting the American Red Cross in 1881."

"Yeah, yeah, yeah," Lucy answered. "And we'll still be playing this baseball game in 2081 if we don't get going."

Charlie Brown sat up and, for once, he agreed with Lucy. The bases were loaded, and they still had one out. "Who's up next?"

Oh no! Lucy—the very worst player on the team—was up to bat. Peppermint Patty threw the first pitch…Strike one!

The next pitch was a curve ball and caught Lucy by surprise…Strike two! She might not be the best baseball player, but Lucy wanted her team to win too.

Lucy dug in her heels and gripped the bat tighter. Peppermint Patty sent the ball sailing right over home plate. Lucy swung as hard as she could and…Rats!

Lucy was out, and the game was over. Final score: Peppermint Patty's team: 59. Charlie Brown's team: zero, zip, nada.

"Good grief," Charlie Brown slumped to the ground in disappointment.

But Sally had exciting news to share. "Bases loaded! Did you see me run all the way to third base?"

Didn't Sally get it? They had lost…again. He had to be the worst team manager of the worst team ever!

"Who cares?" Charlie Brown muttered with a miserable sigh.

All Charlie Brown wanted to do was sit under a tree and mope. But then Marcie ran up with her new camera.

"What a game, Charlie Brown! Great teamwork!" she exclaimed. "Good thing my trusty camera didn't miss a thing."

Marcie showed Charlie Brown a shot of Woodstock and Snoopy preparing the field. And a shot of Franklin helping Sally carry the heavy water bucket.

There he was, flat on the ground. But look—Peppermint Patty and Linus came to his rescue.

"Look at this one," Marcie showed him a picture of the last play of the game. "Lucy was inches away from a grand slam!"

Marcie and her camera had seen a much different game than Charlie Brown had seen. "It's not whether you win or lose. It's how you play the game!"

"This is just like my favorite photographer, Lewis Hine," Marcie said. "He changed history by telling important stories with his pictures, and now so have I."

Just then, Peppermint Patty called out, "Root beer floats, here we come!"

Did someone say root beer floats? Charlie Brown might not know much about Lewis Hine yet. But root beer floats? That was another story!

"Hey, wait for me!"

Up ahead, Charlie Brown's friends were discussing who to pick for most valuable player. "I vote for me," Lucy suggested.

"I vote that we let the boys decide," Schroeder said. He was only kidding, but the girls were not laughing.

"Guess again, Mozart," Peppermint Patty said. "Susan B. Anthony worked too hard to win voting rights for women. We aren't about to give them up now."

It was a good thing that Linus had another idea.

By the time Charlie Brown got there, his friends had made a decision. "We're ready to announce the most valuable player," Linus said.

That honor usually goes to the player who played the best game. But this time it was going to the most caring player.

"And the winner is Charlie Brown!"

Charlie Brown was so surprised that he almost spilled his root beer float. "I'm not the only one who cares," he said.

"We all care!"

Who Cares, Charlie Brown?

Finally! All of Charlie Brown's hard work and dedication paid off. His team chose him as Most Caring Player of the baseball game. What an honor! The Peanuts gang learned about other people—real heroes—who cared so much that they changed the world. They want to share those stories with you.

Who Cares, Franklin?

Martin Luther King Jr.

"The time is always right to do what is right."
—Martin Luther King Jr.

IF I CANNOT DO GREAT THINGS LIKE DR. KING, I CAN DO SMALL THINGS IN A GREAT WAY.

"I have a dream…" Martin Luther King Jr. shared this famous speech with the world back in 1963. His words helped move the American civil rights movement forward. Those same words still inspire people today. At the time, black people were often treated differently than white people. They were not allowed to share the same schools and other types of public places. This was not fair. But for a long time that was how things were.

Dr. King was a preacher. He knew how to use words to change minds. He spoke out against discrimination, and people everywhere listened. It was a long, hard struggle that eventually cost Dr. King his life. He was standing on the balcony of a motel in Memphis on April 4, 1968, when a gunman shot and killed him.

Even a bullet could not stop Dr. King's dream of equal rights for everyone. Our Declaration of Independence says it plain and clear. "All men are created equal." How can equal people not have equal rights? Sometimes people forget. So I'm glad Dr. King still helps us to remember.

Who Cares, Sally?

Rosa Parks

"I would like to be known as a person who is concerned about freedom and equality and justice and prosperity for all people."

—Rosa Parks

My friend Franklin told me about a really brave lady named Rosa Parks. One day she was riding a public bus. She was tired and just wanted to get home from work. She paid her fare and took a seat at the back of the bus. The bus was crowded and there were no empty seats. When a white man got on board, the bus driver told Mrs. Parks to give the man her seat. You see, Rosa Parks was a black woman. Back then the law said that black people had to give up their seats to white people. But Mrs. Parks was tired of giving in all the time. She knew someone had to take the first step to put a stop to this unfair law. This time she said "no"— even though it meant she would get arrested.

> SOME PEOPLE STAND UP FOR THEIR RIGHTS. ROSA PARKS SAT DOWN FOR HERS.

It took a lot of courage to do what she did. She inspired thousands of people to stand up, sit in, and speak out for freedom. It started a movement to make it illegal to discriminate against people because of the color of their skin, gender, religion, or national origins. Years later, Rosa Parks was given the Presidential Medal of Freedom. She is still honored today as the "Mother of the Civil Rights Movement."

NOTHING SAYS "I CARE" LIKE A WARM BLANKET.

Who Cares, Linus?

Clara Barton

"I may be compelled to face danger, but never fear it."

—Clara Barton

Clara Barton was a teacher when most teachers were men. She was one of the first female workers in the federal government. When the Civil War broke out, many wounded soldiers were brought to town. Clara could not just sit behind a desk. She had to help!

As the war raged on, Clara learned there was an even greater need on the battlefields. Soon she was tending wounded soldiers on the front lines at some of the fiercest battles of the war. She was a welcome sight for many a suffering soldier. Clara became known as the "Angel of the Battlefield."

After the war ended, President Abraham Lincoln asked her to help search for missing prisoners of war. Her staff answered over 63,000 letters and identified over 22,000 missing men.

You'd think all this service would be enough for one lifetime. But Clara Barton is even more famous for founding the American Red Cross in 1881. The American Red Cross has helped millions of people in times of war or natural disasters.

I WANT TO BE A CAMERA SPY LIKE MY HERO, LEWIS HINE.

Who Cares, Marcie?

Lewis Hine

"If I could tell the story in words, I wouldn't need to lug around a camera."

—Lewis Hine

There was a time when many poor children were sent to work instead of school. I know it's hard to believe. But it is true. They often worked long hours in dangerous conditions for very little money. These kids worked hard for up to twelve hours a day, six days a week. Lewis Hine knew this was wrong. He quit his teaching job and set out with his camera to uncover the ugly truth about child labor.

He traveled around the country taking pictures of children working in coal mines, textile mills, meat packing houses, and canneries. Factory managers did not want Hine nosing around taking pictures, so he had to work undercover—kind of like a camera spy! He would sneak into factories and take pictures of what he saw. When he talked to the children, he would scribble notes with his hand inside his pocket so no one saw what he was doing.

People were shocked when they saw his photographs. They demanded that children be treated better. It took time, but laws were changed. Finally, kids got to be kids again in America.

I WONDER IF SUSAN B. ANTHONY LIKED BASEBALL?

Who Cares, Peppermint Patty?

Susan B. Anthony

"Independence is happiness..."

—Susan B. Anthony

Susan B. Anthony was a fighter. She fought to end slavery (this was called the abolition movement). She fought to stop the abuse of alcohol (this was called the temperance movement). She is most famous for fighting for women's right to vote (this was called the suffrage movement). These fights were not like wars with weapons. She used words to right what she believed was wrong.

In the 1800s women did not share the same rights as men. They were expected to take care of their homes and families. Married women were not allowed to own property, keep their own wages, or sign contracts. There's really no other way to say it—women were second-class citizens.

Susan B. Anthony spent more than sixty years of her life working to win equal rights for women. She traveled the country making speeches. She wrote many papers calling for change. Women finally won the right to vote in 1920. It is sad that Susan B. Anthony died before that happened.

Who Cares, Reader?
Describe it!
Write a story about something you care about.
(Woodstock says to make sure you use a separate piece of paper if this book doesn't belong to you.)

Who Cares, Reader?

Show it!

Draw a picture of how you can change the world.

(Woodstock says to make sure you use a separate piece of paper if this book doesn't belong to you.)